Touch of Trouble

A Novella

The Blake Brothers Trilogy

Book 2.5

Susan Sey

Other Titles by Susan Sey

The Money Books
MONEY, HONEY
MONEY SHOT

KISS THE GIRL

The Blake Brothers Trilogy
TASTE FOR TROUBLE
TALENT FOR TROUBLE

For the Red Door Reads ladies. I'm proud to be one of you.

For Ben Skrewd, whom we have all found inspirational to one degree or another.

And for Claudia and Greta, in whom the awesome is strong.

Chapter 1

January, Northern Virginia
4:45 a.m.

When it came to trouble, Andrew Blake was kind of an expert. A connoisseur. He was a Blake, after all, and Blakes didn't dabble. When Drew and his brothers went after something, they went after it. Full-bore, whole-hog, balls-out *after* it.

Which was why his middle brother James was a world-class athlete instead of a barstool hero reliving his high school glory days after every shift.

Which was why his oldest brother Will was eating lawyers for breakfast, team owners for lunch, and corporations for dinner instead of picking fights from the barstool next to James'.

Which was why Drew's ass was under arrest.

Again.

"I wish you'd trust me, Meg," he said to the woman beside him. They sat on conjoined plastic chairs in a squat, fluorescent police station that smelled strongly of coffee and vaguely of pee. "We're going to be fine."

"We're *under arrest*, Drew." Meghan Wise blasted him with a brilliant, scathing smile that sent equal measures of fear and lust chasing across his weary brain. "Explain to me again how that equals fine?"

He considered his options. That smile of hers was weapons-grade, no matter if she meant to flatter or flatten with it. He didn't imagine she was after flattering him at this time.

"Arrested isn't charged, kiddo." He sent her a confident

grin and patted her knee. Her eyes dropped to his hand and he snatched it back. There was confident and there was stupid. He was no super-genius—that was Will's department—but nobody had ever called him stupid.

"Arrested comes right before charged," Meg informed him brightly. "Locked up comes in between."

She threw a pointed glance at a door standing open on the facing wall, affording them a fine view of an old-fashioned holding cell complete with metal bars. A guy in a rumpled suit lay on the bench seat running along the back wall of the cell, open-mouthed and snoring like a chain saw.

"What, in there?" Drew snorted. "That's the drunk tank."

"How would you know?" She didn't bother to look at him when she spoke. She kept her eyes firmly on the ugly faux-wooden desk between them and the drunk tank, that just-try-me jaw of hers adorably set. "Do you come here often? Is this your home jail?"

"Actually, yeah," he said. "It sort of is."

Now she did look at him. Stared, really. And this time that sharp prickle of lust lifted the hair on his arms. He liked everything about this girl—that long, silky ponytail she wore all high and tight, that funny pixie nose stranded like an island of whimsy in a strong-boned face, those endless legs. (God, the legs.) But it was the eyes that really did it to him. Green as broken glass and just as sharp, they snapped with skepticism, and—even better—the brains to back it up. And when she focused on him—really focused, not just viewed and dismissed him the way she usually did? Well, it was the thinking man's version of porn. And Drew was in grave danger of addiction.

Then she rolled her eyes. And Drew was dismissed.

"Oh, right. I forgot." She shook her head and pressed those curvy lips flat. Went back to staring at Chief Wharton's ugly desk. "You and your idiot brothers get arrested all the time."

"Hey, now," Drew said mildly. Because he and his brothers *were* idiots, and they *did* get arrested pretty regularly. Used to, anyway. Then his brothers had gone and

2

grown up, dragging Drew along for the ride whether he was ready or not. As usual. But nobody was allowed to bag on the family. Not even girls whose legs went on forever and whose smiles yanked wires loose in a guy's head. "We haven't so much as set foot in a strip club since last year, let alone the drunk tank."

"It's January," she informed him. "Give it a minute."

"We're reformed." Even he could hear the wistfulness in his voice. Meg ignored him, her attention fixed on Chief Wharton who chose that moment to amble over. He lowered himself into the office chair on the other side of that ugly desk with a grunt that spoke to his forty or so years of keeping the peace in northern Virginia's fox-hunt-and-horses country. Or maybe to the forty or so extra pounds on his frame, most of it packed into a tight pot-belly so perfectly spherical that Drew always had to remind himself not to stare.

"Reformed," Wharton said thoughtfully. "You know, I'd heard that." He slid a manila folder onto the desk between them. "Figured it for an ugly rumor."

"Gospel truth," Drew told him. "And you can take that to the bank."

"Oh I will." His luxurious mustache twitched. "Soon as Jerry pays up."

Drew cocked a brow. "You bet on us?"

Wharton pinned him with flat cop eyes. "Do I look like a fool to you, son?"

"No, sir." Drew clamped down on a grin. Wharton was a ball buster. Drew liked him.

"Good." Wharton linked his fingers over that belly and leaned back until his chair complained. "I bet against you."

"Smart man," Meg muttered.

"Jerry thought you'd make it to Groundhogs Day." He didn't grin but his eyes warmed up to a near-twinkle. "I had a twenty that said you wouldn't."

Drew sighed. "Where is Jerry, anyway?"

"Knee replacement, first of the year."

"The bum knee was a real thing?" Drew frowned. "I thought he just liked to talk about his Desert Storm days."

"Little of one, little of the other. Then some ladies came to blows down at Maxwell's and he took a hard knee in a spilled mojito."

"Bad luck." Which it was. For Jerry *and* for Drew, as it had evidently resulted in Wharton hiring the Dudley Do-Right who'd arrested them and was now busily filling out forms at the booking desk up front. "How's the recovery coming?"

"Slow." Wharton flipped open the folder on the desk between them. There was a stack of paper inside a full inch thick. Wharton pinched the bridge of his nose. "Or maybe it just seems that way."

Drew cast a sidelong look toward the new deputy, all military hair and ramrod spine, carefully checking boxes and filling in blanks. "Captain America likes his paperwork, does he?"

"Some do. Takes all kinds." Wharton dropped his hand and met Drew's eyes. "Then again? Guy's going to have himself quite a shiner come morning." The chief's gaze was steady on Drew, heavy. Like a hand on his shoulder. Drew ordered himself not to shift in his chair like a guilty kid. "You want to tell me what the *hell* went down out there tonight?"

"Ah..." Drew cast a furtive glance Meg's way, wondering exactly how much of the truth it would take to get them out of this. He figured he knew. Just like he knew that that much truth would destroy any chance he might've had at seeing the lovely Meghan naked. Regret sat heavy in his stomach. He'd really wanted to see her naked. She refused to meet his eyes.

Finally he said, "It's sort of a long story, Chief."

Wharton flicked his gaze toward Happy McHandcuffs at the booking desk. He sighed. "I got time, son. Fill me in."

Chapter 2

Four Hours Earlier

Drew threw his old Blazer into reverse and backed out of the drive. Meg swallowed against the hot bundle of nerves trying to crawl up her throat and clicked her seatbelt into place. She watched her mom back out of the drive in front of them. Watched her put the pedal down and rocket out of the dark cul de sac in a cloud of worry and haste.

"Whoa," Drew said. He punched the clutch, shoved the gear shift into first and peeled out after her. "Easy there, Hildy," he murmured as if her mom could hear him. He hit second before they'd even cleared the circle. "These here are residential streets."

"Just keep up." Meg leaned forward and unzipped the black backpack between her feet. Pulled out the familiar kit and started arming herself with tiny cameras and recording devices. "I don't want her to get ahead of us."

"On it." Drew narrowed his eyes and glued himself to her mom's bumper until they'd left behind the subdivision and the family who lived there. The family Meg's mom had just fixed. Then there was nothing but night between them and the next family in crisis.

Which her mother wouldn't be fixing. Not tonight. Not ever. Not that she'd stop trying.

Meg pressed a hand to her jumping stomach and put the nerves away. The ache in her heart would never stop—she knew this from bitter experience—so she didn't bother trying to push it in behind the nerves. She just threw a smile on top of it. A slick, shiny one. Her specialty.

They hit the highway, and Drew relaxed enough to slide

her a look across the dark truck. "So," he said. "Where are we going?"

Meg spared him a single glance. He was tall and lanky, his hair a nut-brown bramble that brushed the ceiling of the car and spoke to the fact that she'd busted into his room and dragged him out of bed not ten minutes ago. His face was an odd collection of mobile lines and sharp angles, lit from below by the soft glow of the dash. He looked like nothing so much as a cartoon. An appealing cartoon, but a cartoon nonetheless.

"Not that I care." He sent her a smile of melting adoration. "Anywhere with you is good by me."

"Oh for God's sake." She gathered her hair into a high ponytail, yanked it through the holder until it was tight enough to feel like a face lift. And to give the tiny recording devices buried in her earrings a fighting chance. "Pull yourself together, Drew."

"I'm trying, pretty Meg." He gave her one last soulful gaze and turned his attention back to the road. "I've been trying for two days. But you've upset my apple cart."

"Do you want me to vomit on the floor boards?"

"Uh, no."

"Then knock it off."

"Right."

They drove in silence for a few minutes, Drew's big hands easy on the wheel despite the speedometer flirting with ninety. Everything about Drew was outsized—the hands, the height, the hair, the emotions that made such a cartoon of his face. She'd expected him to take up the challenge of her mom's reckless speed with the glee of a teenage boy, and he had.

To be fair, it couldn't have been all that long ago that he *had* been a teenage boy. If he had more than a year or two on her own twenty, Meg would eat the audio recorder riding in her bra. But he handled the wheel with an easy competence, matching her Mom's barn-burning pace with a nonchalance that made her wonder how fast he usually drove.

"So if I'm not supposed to ask where we're going, am I at least allowed to ask why I'm going with you?" He didn't look at her this time, just kept an eye on her mom's tail lights like a good boy. "Because if you wanted to ignore me, the least you could've done was let me sleep through it."

Meg pulled out her smart phone and checked the feed on all her recorders. She was live. She zipped the case, slipped it back into the bag between her feet and sat up. Pressed herself into the seat and filled her lungs for the first time in half an hour.

"I wanted to ask Will," she told him. "Mom insisted on you."

"I figured." He sighed. "Moms love me."

"Of course they do." Meg couldn't deny him that truth. He was ridiculously charming. Utterly harmless and absolutely without edges. But charming. "Everybody loves you."

He made a sad mouth. "Everybody but you."

"Everybody but me."

"And why is that again?" He shot her a longing look. "What's not to love here, Meg? I'm a decent guy. I'm a college graduate, I'm gainfully employed, I'm taller than you—which, let's be frank, can't be an easy find—and I don't have a single problem with a girl who can pin cable better than I can."

She snorted. "My grandma pins cable better than you."

He smiled easily. "It's my kryptonite."

"Now you're Superman?"

"Nope. I'm just the guy who's dying to know what you think you're going to be recording with your bra tonight."

"Probably nothing." Meg's amusement vanished. "It's just a precaution."

"Against what? Are your breasts fomenting revolution?"

"My breasts are none of your business."

"Oh, Meg." He smiled indulgently at the darkness outside the windshield. "I'm a guy. Everybody's breasts are my business."

"So your interest in my breasts isn't personal?"

"Of course it's personal. Revolutionary breasts are hard to come by. But you don't need to resort to surveillance

7

devices. I'd be happy to keep eye on them for you."

"I'm sure you would." A grin tugged at the corners of her mouth, and the headache that had been threatening for the past half hour eased off a degree or two. Drew was as impossible to dislike as he was to take seriously. "I've got the situation in hand, however."

"No, please," he said solemnly. "Leave it in *my* hands."

She sighed. "Do you ever give it a rest?"

"I'm a guy," he said again. "I can't."

"Try."

Another few minutes of silence. Drew followed her mom onto an exit ramp, through a progressively darker tangle of twisted streets and finally into the moneyed countryside outside DC.

"Okay, I have to know," Drew said. "Where on earth are we going?"

Hildy's brake lights flashed and she skidded into a drive marked *private* without the benefit of her blinker. Drew followed without twitching a lash. The truck slid into the abrupt turn like a car commercial. He didn't even brush the tall hedges standing guard on either side. They crested a little berm and Meg pointed.

A two story colonial stood at the end of the drive, light pouring from every window. The front door stood open and she could hear the shouting through the truck windows. The *closed* truck windows.

"There," she said, her stomach cold, her palms slippery. "We're going there."

Chapter 3

Hildy had already bailed out of her little compact by the time Drew skidded to a halt beside it. In the three seconds it took him to kill the engine and yank the parking brake, she'd scurried up the front steps and disappeared through the open front door. He frowned after her, then turned to Meg to ask yet again what the hell was going on here.

Only to find himself addressing thin air.

Well, shit. Meg had bailed out, too. He spun back to his window and saw her bee-lining for the house. That straight, silky ponytail tick-tocked between tight shoulder blades, and when she hit the veranda she didn't break stride. She simply gathered herself and took the steps in a single fluid leap like some kind of glossy racehorse. Drew suffered an automatic tingle of lust—Jesus, those *legs*—then an equally compelling tingle of curiosity. He really, really wanted to know what was going on here.

He threw himself out of the Blazer, pocketed the keys and started after her. Then he stopped and jogged back to the truck. He grabbed Meg's backpack from the floor boards and tossed it over his shoulder before hustling after her. He'd learned early and young that you didn't leave anything behind. There was no telling when—or even if—you might be back. He ate dessert first, too. Why take chances?

He took the porch steps by easy twos and helped himself to the open front door. He found Meg in a nice foyer—lots of white woodwork and pretty colors, with a set of wide stairs giving out onto a thick rug that he could tell didn't belong in a museum but probably hadn't come from Target either. Drew made the assessment as automatically as he'd grabbed the backpack. You couldn't carry everything; it paid to ID the valuables ahead of time.

Raised voices poured down from above like a raging river. Meg hesitated on the landing like she was steeling herself to struggle upstream against them. Drew's heart gave an odd bump and he shut the front door behind him.

"You're welcome, sleeping neighbors," he said lightly.

Meg snapped out of that grim contemplation and sent him a sideways smile. "Yeah, thanks," she said. "But I think they're used to it."

"Not your mom's first house call here?"

"Hardly."

He cocked a cautious ear to the inchoate rage pouring down the stairs. Hildy Wise was the most famous ghost buster in the tri-state area. Drew wasn't sure exactly what she charged but he felt certain it was more than these modest rug-owners could comfortably afford. "Must be one hell of a haunting if they're willing to shell out for your mom."

"The house isn't haunted," Meg said. She stripped off her jacket, hung it on the newel post and set off up the stairs with her usual brisk determination.

"Okay." Drew looped the backpack over her jacket, tossed his own jacket after it and fell in behind her. A collection of framed photos marched up the wall to his left, all of a young woman. "Hey, is this our screamer?"

Meg glanced back and he pointed his chin to the photos. The girl in the frame closest to the foyer was probably within a year or two of Drew's own age, serious and pale under a mortar-board cap and tassel.

Meg's mouth tightened. "That's her."

"Pretty."

"Understatement," she said and kept climbing. She was right, of course. This girl was a knock-out. Inky hair, moonlight skin, anime-sized eyes and a sweetly tragic mouth. Drew kept an eye on the photos as he climbed, noticed how they shed years with each riser. By the time he neared the top, the girl was just a kid. Eleven? Twelve? Far too young to look so terribly grave and sober-eyed.

"What's her issue?" he asked.

"Depends on the night," Meg said. She stopped at the

10

top of the steps to wait for him. "And who you ask."

The final picture was of the girl with both skinny arms lashed around a dog the size of a small pony.

"Hey, look at that," Drew said, touching the frame. "Little Miss Serious finally cracked a smile." Happiness radiated from the picture so palpably that Drew grinned just looking at it. Even the dog was smiling, tongue lolling out the side of a big, goofy dog-grin. But it was the girl who really nailed Drew between the eyes, smiling into the camera with such fierce delight. It hit him like a hammer, like a punch he hadn't been ready for. His mouth fell open and he gaped at Meg.

Who wasn't smiling, but it didn't matter. Because he'd seen that smile before, the one in the photo. He'd *been* seeing it to the exclusion of all else for the past two days. That was Meg's own smile this girl was wearing. This wasn't Meg but that was her smile, no question.

"Holy shit," he breathed and Meg's shoulders went up nearly to her ears. She turned on her heel and stalked off down the hall. Drew scrambled after her. "Meg, who *is* she?"

Those long, long legs took her down the runner and into an open door before Drew could catch her but he didn't need an answer. He already knew. That smile had gone off in his brain like an atomic bomb and the fallout was showering gently down in his mind like nuclear snow.

This was Meg's sister. She couldn't be anything else. Which meant that this middle-of-the-night flight wasn't a house call. This wasn't Hildy Wise, psychic, harmlessly de-ghosting somebody's attic. This was a family crisis. This was *Meg's* family crisis.

What the *hell* was he doing here?

It surprised her every time. Meg had personally witnessed her sister Clara melt down more times than she could count and she was always left with a single insistent question: How could somebody so small break so much shit?

"Whoa." Drew stopped in the doorjamb next to her, awe in his voice as he took it in. "Meg, what should we—"

"Nothing. Not yet. Mom's talking her down. Let it play

out for a minute." Meg set her jaw and turned her head, carefully letting her earrings record the destruction. "One twenty-two a.m. Drew and I arrived approximately five minutes ago. Mom was no more than a minute ahead of us. I'm seeing clothes out of the drawers, drawers overturned on the floor." She narrated for the recorder in her bra, hoping it could catch her voice over Clara's enraged wailing. "Top of the dresser swept clean, perfume bottle smashed on the floor—"

"No kidding," Drew said, pulling his t-shirt up over his nose. "I know that's probably expensive but holy crap my eyes are watering."

"—books out of the case, pages torn out, suitcase upended, curtains ripped down, closet rod out, clothes thrown." She paused to swallow down a hard lump of anger and grief. "It looks like the mattress was pulled off the bed at some point, probably by the sheets. Clara's lying across it on the floor, significantly escalated. Maybe an hour or two into the episode, judging by her usual cycle."

Such clinical, precise words. Meg marveled at the way they managed to capture the event while avoiding even a whiff of the madness driving it. Because the truth was that Clara was sprawled across the beached mattress, face-up, screaming her throat raw. Her hands were twisted in the sheets like claws, the better to anchor herself while she beat her heels against the wadded comforter in slow, savage strokes—one, *two*, one, *two*—and howled.

On and on it went, tears spurting from her screwed-shut eyes. Red splotches stained her cheeks in perfect circles, and she looked like nothing so much as a thwarted fairy queen, her beauty only heightened by the rage.

Meg's parents stood on either side of the mattress, gazing down at their troubled daughter, a study in opposites. Hildy was small and soft, radiating receptive compassion like a loving little space heater. Meg's dad, on the other hand, stood tall and stiff, as if endurance were the same thing as patience. But Meg could see the baffled love in his eyes. She had to give him that much. Joe Marshall loved his kid.

But she wouldn't give him another inch, because for his

12

ex-wife? For the mother of his children? He had nothing but blame and anger. Which was ironic, considering that much of the blame for the mess at his feet—both literally and figuratively—was his.

"What triggered her?" Hildy murmured, absorbing Clara's rage with her usual serenity.

"College," Joe said shortly. "She'd like to go."

Hildy's brows lifted. "Isn't she in college?"

"She's taking a few courses at Loudon Community." Joe paused. "Evidently, she'd like to go away to college."

"Ah." Hildy pulled in a long breath. "Where?"

"I don't care!" Clara wailed. "I just want to go *away*! I hate it here. I hate *him!* I hate *being* here, being this *way*. I want something *else*—"

Joe ignored this with weary determination and continued speaking to Hildy. "Unclear. But she'd like to go as soon as possible. Tonight, preferably."

"Oh dear." Hildy's eyes filled with pain and sympathy.

"You can't keep me here," Clara howled. "You have no *right*! I'm not a child. I'm twenty years old! I'm a legal *adult*! And adults go to *college!*"

"Clara, sweetheart, listen to me," Joe began.

Drew winced and muttered, "Don't do it, buddy."

Meg frowned at him. "Don't do what?"

"Play the logic card." He shook his head. "I don't know what that girl's issue is, but I can tell you right now that if that guy right there?" He nodded Joe's way.

"That would be my dad."

"I figured. Can I call him Dad?"

"You can call him Joe. I do."

"Really?"

"Really."

"Huh. Okay. Well if our buddy Joe tries to talk reason to..." He drifted off, gave her an eyebrow prompt.

"Clara," Meg supplied. "My twin."

"Your *twin*? Wow." Drew gave that information a brief head shake but offered no further comment. Meg was glad. Nobody had ever mistaken *her* for a fairy queen—enraged or otherwise—and she'd gotten tired of that conversation years ago. "Well, anyway, Joe's about to buy himself another ride on the Scary-Go-Round."

Meg stared. "What makes you say?"

"Because the last thing a crying woman wants to hear is reason. She's *feeling* shit, you know? You want to get through to a weeper? You don't play the logic card. Jesus." Drew gave her the side eye. "You're a girl, Meg. Don't you know this already?"

Back at the mattress, Hildy said, "Joe, stop. You'll only make it worse."

Drew smiled at Meg. Smugly. "See? Your mom knows." He shook his head. "You're going to get your girl card revoked, pretty Meg."

Pretty Meg. Nobody had ever called her pretty, and for good reason. She wished Drew would knock it off. She didn't have the reserves to deal with that crap tonight. Not when she was too busy being the useful, stable, *logical* twin. Not to mention the huge, ugly one.

"What would I want with a girl card?" She gave him a shiny, impenetrable smile. "I already got dealt all this smart and ambitious, and a pair of long, long legs to boot. Anything more would be greedy."

Drew leaned in, his eyes on her smile. On her lips. "Greedy can be fun, though. Really, really fun. Don't you think?"

Her pulse gave an interested thud and she rolled her eyes. At him, sure. But also at herself. Because sex wasn't fun. It was more like exercise. Sweaty, awkward, embarrassing, and often exchanged for strength and power. It was a testament to Drew's charm that he could pull any interest from her at all, let alone *now*.

"This is hardly the moment, Drew."

He cleared his throat and looked away. "Jeez. Of course it's not. I know that. It's just...Damn, Meg. I don't think straight when you smile at me."

She wanted to cover her eyes but knew it would only obscure the earring cameras. "Please just shut up and stand by. I might need you to get between them."

"Between who? Joe and Clara?"

14

"Joe and Mom."

"Cripes, really?"

She moved unobtrusively into the room to get a better angle for the video. "Really."

He followed her like a very tall shadow. "This explains why you wanted Will. My brother is aces in a bar fight."

"I figured. I said as much to Mom. She wanted you instead. She likes your energy."

Drew grinned. I *am* pretty energetic. I'd love to show you sometime."

"Just shut up and be ready, okay?"

"Oh, Meg." His voice brimmed with laughter. "I'm *always* ready."

"Of course you are." Meg sighed. She'd walked into that one. "Maybe you could focus on the shutting up part?"

"As you wish, pretty Meg." He gave her another dose of the big soulful eyes, and she realized that he was quoting the *Princess Bride* again. He'd been doing it for two days now. Long enough for her to know that every time Westley said those words to his beloved Princess Buttercup, he'd really been saying *I love you*. Drew leaned in earnestly. "*As you wish.*"

Nerves gave a sudden twitch inside her. Sex was one thing; love was something else entirely. She didn't know what exactly that *something else* might be, only that Drew shouldn't be joking about it. She scowled at him. "I *wish* you'd shut up, then."

He dropped the earnestness like he'd strip off a sweater and shrugged cheerfully. "Okay."

And he shut up, love as blanked from his mind as yesterday's pizza.

She was glad she'd scowled at him.

15

Chapter 4

Meg turned her back on him, evidently out of patience with banter. Or maybe just with him. Which was too bad, because Drew liked banter. He also liked Meg. And really, things were getting grim in here. These people could use a little banter.

Meg moved toward the rumpled mattress where her sister was throwing the fit to end all fits, and Drew stayed close.

Because he didn't care for this situation. Didn't care for the way Meg was handling it, either. Like it was perfectly normal to find your sister—your *twin* sister—having some kind of break with reality in the middle of the night. Like she was absolutely okay with documenting it instead of responding to it. Like these people were her *job* more than her family.

But, you know, maybe they were. Maybe it was better that way. Because, damn, look at them there. He stopped at Meg's shoulder and followed her gaze to her family. To Joe and Hildy looking helplessly on while their child's fury split their family neatly in half.

Or maybe not so neatly, he thought suddenly, turning his gaze back to Meg. Because three divided by one didn't equal the even teams he was looking at here. So who was *she* in all this? What was Meg's role?

Then he realized that he already knew. Wasn't she doing it right in front of him? There she was, apart from it all. Watching. Waiting. Recording.

His chest went oddly hollow and he only just stopped himself from touching one of those stiff, brave shoulders. She wouldn't appreciate the gesture. He didn't know how he

16

knew it, only that it was true. And he regretted again the ban on banter. The situation was going from grim to grimmer, and he'd like to see Meg smile again. Even if only at his expense.

He shifted his attention back to the stand-off in front of them, and wondered who'd cave first. His money was on Joe. Big hands in fists, wide mouth pressed flat, cheekbones standing out like craggy cliffs? Guy looked worn, dangerous, and about out of post-midnight patience.

"Of course you can go to college, sweetheart," Hildy murmured to Clara, but Drew didn't look her way. He kept his eyes on Joe. On those fists of his. "Your father didn't mean—"

"Hildy, don't," Joe snapped, and Drew tensed. Hildy was tough—tough as they came—but she was built like a damn bird. He let his weight come to the balls of his feet, let the idea of violence bubble in his blood. Just a little. "Don't you dare lie to her. She can't go away to college. Look at her!" Joe flung an open hand toward his daughter still howling on the mattress. "She can't handle a simple request to table a discussion until morning. How dare you promise her—"

Hildy didn't even look at him. She simply sank to her knees beside the mattress and gazed at her weeping daughter with such naked compassion that the fight in Drew's veins fizzled and went out. Who could hold onto a mad with all that *love* beaming around?

Evidently, Joe could.

"Christ." He tossed those big, dangerous-looking hands into the air. "Here we go."

"Joe," Meg snapped. "Be quiet."

Her father started as if he'd only just noticed her there. Only just noticed her at all. Probably the story of her childhood, Drew realized. And that was a shame. Nobody should overlook Meg.

"No, Meghan, I won't be quiet. I *refuse* to be quiet." He aimed a finger at her. "Clara has her issues but we're dealing with them. She has the best—"

"—medication and therapists money can buy, I know."

17

Susan Sey

Meg folded her arms and adjusted to keep everybody in the shot. Drew marveled at her ability to think along two separate tracks with such consummate ease. "And yet here we are."

"She's off her meds," Joe said tightly.

"Of course she is," Meg returned. "Because that's what she does when you mess with her."

Joe made a disgusted noise. "Not this again."

Meg only smiled, brilliantly. "Believe me, I don't want to say it any more than you want to hear it. But you're giving me no choice here. Either you give Clara what she wants or she gives you—" Meg cast a significant glance at Clara raging on the floor. At Hildy kneeling at her side, knitting words together like a soft blanket to lay over her daughter's fury. "—this."

"She's ill, Meghan, not selfish or spoiled." Joe's eyes were green and cold. "And to imply that she is—"

"—would be selfish and spoiled of *me*." Meg smiled again, brighter this time. "Touché."

Joe's silence was damning and that little thread of violence uncurled inside Drew again, swam silkily through his veins. He wondered at it. Wondered if this was what it felt like to be Will, all fists and teeth and just-give-me-a-reason.

"Lucky for me, though, I don't give a shit what you think of me," Meg said. "All I want is for you to hear what I'm saying to you. Clara wants Mom. And you can either get on board with that or brace yourself for more—"

"Her mother is a fraud." The *and so are you* was unspoken but Meg jerked back like he'd said it out loud. Like words were fists. And as far as Drew knew, being familiar with the fists didn't stop the bruises. "And indulging Clara's delusions doesn't help her. Not in the end."

"It'll help her tonight," Meg said with admirable cool. "If you'll be quiet and let Mom work."

Joe ignored her, spoke to Hildy on the floor. "Touch her and I'll call the police."

Drew blinked at Meg. "Police?"

Meg turned that smile on him, and it was tight and hard

18

and bright. "Joe took out a restraining order."

Drew looked back at Joe. "You took out a restraining order against your kid's mom?" he asked, honestly baffled. Drew wasn't a dumb guy. He couldn't compete with Will's dizzying IQ, but against anybody else? He held his own, and then some. But his mind refused to process the fact—no, the very *concept*—of erecting a legal barrier between family members.

Joe met his eyes for the first time. Probably just noticed him there, too. Sandy brows came down hard, and Drew felt the full impact of those ruthless green eyes. Same color as Meg's, and about as interested in him. Nice.

Joe snapped, "Who the hell are you?"

"Drew Blake." He didn't offer a hand. "I'm this evening's muscle."

Joe gave him a dismissive up-and-down. Yep, Meg's eyes were definitely this guy's fault. "If you say so."

Drew shrugged easily. "I have a subtle build."

"I'm sure that's effective."

"You'd be surprised."

"I don't intend to be."

Drew grinned, enjoying himself now. "Who does?"

Joe turned back to Hildy. "If you touch her, I swear on all that's holy, I'm calling 911."

Hildy didn't touch anything. She simply lifted her palms to Clara, like her howling daughter was a crackling fire and Hildy was feeling chilly. She closed her eyes and tipped her head. A line of deep concentration appeared between her fine eyebrows and she leaned in, like she was hearing something nobody else could. Like she was spinning the dial on some internal radio, searching for the right signal.

It wasn't the first time Drew had seen her do this. He'd watched her do it yesterday morning for a teammate of James', a Spanish goalie who believed somebody had put the hoodoo on him or something. Yesterday night, he'd watched her do it for the little girl his brother Will was about to raise as his own, if Drew wasn't mistaken.

And, cripes, wasn't that another mind-boggler? William Blake, the guy-most-likely when it came to fisticuffs—and to winning said fisticuffs—was about to become a family man. And seemed damn happy about it. Drew had *not* seen that one coming.

It only went to show you, he supposed. Life was a wild and unpredictable ride. Developing expectations was just begging Fate for a rabbit punch. Which was why Drew believed in remaining open to the possibility. The possibility of what? Of anything, really. His childhood had been one long rabbit punch, starting with fifth grade and the car wreck that had stolen his folks. He wasn't really in the market for more.

So it wasn't that he believed Hildy could commune with spirits. It was more that he had no reason to disbelieve it. He himself had never experienced even a whiff of anything paranormal but that didn't mean it didn't exist. Truth was a fluid thing, and pinning shit down that wanted to move was just asking for trouble. And not the kind of trouble Drew traditionally enjoyed.

So when Hildy started dialing into her ghost-station, or whatever it was she did when she closed her eyes and reached out like this? Drew didn't judge. He shut up and paid attention. Because you just never knew, did you?

Joe, however? Tense as a drawn bow, phone in hand? He looked like the judgy type. He wasn't dialing, though. Just waiting. Drew got the feeling that Joe was a man of his word, and that those words were habitually precise. The instant Hildy laid hands on this girl, Joe would start punching numbers. Until she did, though, he'd hold. But he'd be ready. He probably *wasn't* surprised very often. What a sad way to live.

Back on the mattress, Clara's head lashed side to side on the tangled sheets and she wailed, her rage beyond words. Hildy just breathed and murmured and after several long moments, Clara's volume began to drop. Drew watched with interest as the girl's legs went still, then her hands relaxed. Her face was last to let the anger go, but he watched it drift away from each perfect feature, drop by drop, until her brow went smooth and her sobs dwindled to weary sniffles.

"There now, darling," Hildy murmured, and drew her

hands back. She laid them on her knees, open and spent, and sat back on her heels. There were lines on her face, deeper and plainer than before, and Drew wondered again what exactly she did. What it cost her. Meg's mouth was a tight line, her eyes hard on her sister.

"She'll rest now," Hildy told Joe and went to rise. Meg was at her side instantly, a hand under her elbow, her back to her father. Joe stuffed his phone into his back pocket, and relief chased frustration over his face.

"Damn it, Hildy. You can't keep doing this," he said. "It's not fair to her, and it isn't helping."

"What's the alternative?" Hildy asked evenly. "You can't force her to take the meds. She's going to be twenty-one next month—"

"I know." Joe's cheekbones stood out starkly in the overhead light. "Believe me, I know. I've applied for a conservatorship."

"But that's a long shot and you know it," Hildy said, her voice worn. Like she'd been screaming, too, though Drew knew she'd never raised her voice above a whisper. "She's not proven herself a danger, Joe. Not to herself or to others."

"Not proved it, no." Joe pinched the bridge of his nose and closed his eyes. When he opened them, they were clear and focused but full of sorrow. "But do we really want to her to?" He held Hildy's gaze without flinching. "Do we really want to risk it? To risk *her*?"

Hildy's silence was heavy and resigned. "No," she said finally. "We don't." She folded her hands into one another in front of her neatly pressed trousers and nodded once. "We should talk," she said. "In the kitchen."

Joe hesitated. "Clara?"

"Will sleep for a time yet." Hildy smiled. "Trust me."

"Trust the magic? The spirits?" Joe's mouth twisted. "I don't think so." He looked at Meg. "Stay with your sister."

Meg looked back, her face utterly blank, her eyes just as green and just as hard as her father's.

"Please," Drew said.

All eyes swung his way but he met Joe's. Only Joe's.

"You forgot to say please," Drew pointed out

reasonably. "I'm sure it was an oversight. What with the restraining order and all."

Temper tightened the skin across those sharp bones but Joe shifted his eyes back to Meg. "Will you please make sure Clara doesn't wake up alone?"

"Of course," Meg said. She smiled slickly. "And if the cops come, I'll make sure to let them know I had your permission."

"Meg," Hildy murmured and gave her head a small shake. Meg jerked one shoulder but went scowling to the naked box spring and sat down. Hildy nodded Joe toward the door. "Shall we? I'll make tea."

"Tea. Sure." Joe gave Clara a last look, and Drew could almost smell the anguish on him. Meg, though? Joe didn't look her way again. "There's whisky over the fridge. Be generous with mine."

"If you wish." Hildy glided past him into the hallway.

"Christ, Hildy." Joe stomped after her. "Enough judging."

"I didn't say a word."

"You don't need to. A guy doesn't need to be a psychic to know when his wife's judging him."

"Ex-wife." Her reply floated off down the hallway.

Drew just caught Joe's harsh laugh as they headed for stairs. "Like I could forget."

Their voices tangled together and trailed off as they descended, and Drew lost the thread.

"It'll go on like that for a while," Meg told him. She sat on the edge of the box spring, her long legs folded up until she could rest her chin on her knees. She wrapped her arms around her shins and gazed impassively down at her sleeping sister. "Nothing will get resolved. Nothing will change. In a couple of months—weeks, days, years, whatever—we'll be right back to this. Fighting over Sleeping Beauty here." She nudged the mattress with her foot. "They're downstairs, by the way," she said to her sacked out twin. "Olly olly oxen free."

Clara's long, dark lashes fluttered beautifully on the rise of her flushed cheekbones. They lifted slowly, then drifted shut again. Clara sighed and curled into a sleepy C, both hands tucked under her cheek. Meg kicked the mattress again, put a little more behind it this time. Clara's eyes snapped open.

"Damn it, Meg," she said, and her voice was round and bell-like. As if she'd never screamed a day in her life. "That was nearly my head."

Chapter 5

Meg snorted. "I only wish."

Clara dropped the façade of sleep like a movie star slipping off a mink stole. She sat up and tossed back a few acres of tumbled hair, cutting Drew a doe-eyed glance from beneath those lashes. Meg suddenly wished she'd warned him about Clara. Prepared him or something. Because between the face and the fragility, Clara packed a one-two punch that nothing with a Y chromosome could resist. And Drew's apple cart was easier to upset than most. Or so Meg assumed. Certainly she'd never upset one so easily before.

But Drew was made of sterner stuff than she'd imagined. He simply returned Clara's flirty peep in assessing silence, his brows climbing slowly toward his hairline.

"Huh," he said finally. "Got to say, I did *not* see that one coming."

"No?" Clara twinkled at him, comfortably cross-legged now in her nest of twisted blankets. All that hair spilled down her back like a sheet of night. "Excellent."

Drew looked over her head to Meg. "Is she really off her meds?"

Meg shook her head. "Nope."

"How can you tell?"

Clara frowned at him. Adorably. "Excuse me. I'm right here."

"Please." Meg rolled her eyes. "Elizabeth Taylor didn't chew that much scenery in *Cleopatra*."

"I beg your pardon." Clara put her regal little nose in the air. "I do *not* chew scenery."

Drew grinned delightedly. "I loved Liz as Cleopatra."

Meg fought an answering grin. "You would."

"She won an Oscar for that role," Clara put in peevishly.

"No, that was *Who's Afraid Of Virginia Woolf.*" Meg told her. "And she chewed it up in that one, too." She pushed to her feet. "So, Drew. This is my sister Clara."

"Her *twin* sister." Clara rose with her usual tidy grace and dimpled up at him. "She leaves that part out."

"I can't imagine why," Meg muttered, and her stomach knotted. Because surely the dimples would do it. They'd upset Drew's apple cart, no problem, and she didn't know why she was dreading it. She ought to just get it over with. Let Clara spill those apples, let her dive into them like a goddamn ball pit. She could make cider out of them for all Meg cared. Whatever. It would hardly be the first time a guy had gotten a load of Meg's *twin* and switched teams. She just wanted it done.

"You don't need to be mean," Clara said to Meg, her dimples dimming. "I'm crazy, not contagious."

Drew grinned down at her. "You're not even crazy," he told her. "Just manipulative, devious and ruthless."

Clara's eyes went wide and shocked, then her gaze dropped. Her lip trembled. Just the bottom one. Meg had no idea how she did that. Poor Drew. He didn't stand a chance.

"You're very, very good at it, too," Drew told her cheerfully. Even admiringly. "I can't wait to see what you pull out for an encore."

Clara's brows snapped together and she turned narrowed eyes on Meg. "Who is this again?"

Meg hesitated. She was starting to wonder that herself, actually. "This is Drew Blake."

"Huh." Clara considered this. "And he's your...what?"

"Muscle." Drew held out a friendly hand. "I'm her muscle. For tonight, anyway."

She gave his hand an absent shake. She gave that long, lean body a skeptical once over. "Her muscle, huh?"

Drew sighed. "Why is everybody so surprised by that?"

"Don't take it personally," Meg advised him, an unexpected chuckle bubbling up her throat. "You have a subtle build."

"Aw." He grinned at her. "You were paying attention when I was chatting up your dad!"

She shook her head. "No, I was listening. It's different."

"It's a start, pretty Meg." He beamed at her. "It's a start."

The chuckle died before it was born. "Would you please knock it off with that?"

"With what?" To his credit, he looked genuinely confused.

"With all that upset-your-apple-cart business. Your apple cart is fine, and we're having kind of a trying night here. Can we focus, please?"

"Don't listen to her, Drew," Clara said seriously, though Meg could see the smirk in her eyes. "Pretty Meg gets her way too often. You just keep doing whatever you're doing."

Pretty Meg. From Clara, no less. Bitterness rose up in her throat and she took a moment to breathe through it. She returned Clara's smirk with her shiniest, most slippery smile. "Speaking of getting your way too often," she said, "maybe you can let us in on whatever it is you're doing here. The devious plot behind tonight's little drama."

Clara's eyes slid away from hers and she lifted one lazy shoulder. "No plot." She gave a little pout and dropped cross-legged onto the beached mattress again. "Nothing that panned out, anyway."

"What were you hoping for, then?" Drew asked. He walked over to the box spring and lowered himself to the edge. He pushed those long legs out in front of him and leaned comfortably back on his hands. "Mommy and Daddy back in the same room, playing nice for a change?"

"Please." Clara rolled her eyes. "I'll give you two more guesses, then I'll be too bored to carry on."

"Fair enough." Drew tipped his head and studied her. "Well, if it's not family, it's got to be either love or money. And since you appear to be on Daddy's dime still, I'm going with love."

"Love?" She treated him to her profile. "Do I look like the kind of girl who has trouble landing her man?"

"Depends on who you're after, I guess." He sat forward

to scrutinize her more closely, elbows on knees, fingers linked loosely. "Who *are* you after?"

"Who says I'm after anybody?" She gave him a sideways peep, all serious eyes and almost-smile. "Nice girls don't chase boys, you know. And bad girls don't need to."

"Right." Drew nodded slowly. "So who is he?"

"Didn't I just say it wasn't love?"

"I'm after a name here, Clara."

She dropped the ingénue routine to glare at him. "I'm not in love."

"Okay. An older man, maybe?" His eyes went round. "Is it your professor at Loudon Community? Because I have to tell you, that's not going to end well, no matter how many fits you pitch."

"Oh, ick." Clara wrinkled her nose. "Meg likes old men. I can do better."

"Be my guest," Meg said evenly. "But in my experience, anybody under thirty kisses like a cocker spaniel."

"A cocker spaniel?" Drew blinked, eyes bright with laughter.

"Uncontrollable tongue. Paws all over the place," Meg told him. "Tendency to hump the furniture."

"But they get so *hairy* after thirty," Clara said.

"Men or cocker spaniels?" Drew asked.

Both women ignored him. "There *is* that," Meg said. "But there's always something. I'd rather deal with excess hair than indiscriminate humping."

"You wouldn't say that if you'd taken a good look at Dad's eyebrows lately." Clara shuddered. "Good Christ, Meg. It's a cage match to get his reading glasses on."

"I have good eyebrows," Drew offered.

Clara gave him a narrow inspection. "They *are* good," she said.

"Thank you."

"Older men are patient," Meg told him ruthlessly. Because he *did* have good eyebrows. He had good hands, too. He couldn't pin cable worth a damn, but she remembered those hands of his on the wheel. Big, deft, easy.

And now she was starting to wonder, damn it. Starting to wonder what else those hands could do, and whether she'd like to find out. "They don't push and they don't rush. They know how to take their time."

"They know how to take *your* time," Drew told her. "And if they don't ask for anything you don't want to give, it's because they're already getting it." He paused significantly. "From their wives."

"Nice." Clara gave him an approving nod. "You don't pull your punches, do you?"

"Life's short," Drew told her. "Don't lie."

"I'm not lying," Meg said tightly.

"I didn't say you were." He turned back to Clara. "But you are."

"Shut up."

Drew grinned at her. "Mature."

She folded her arms and ignored him. Drew let her. He simply gazed at her, his face open and patient and expectant. Finally she flopped onto her back and let out a muffled shriek. "God! You're like a conversation ninja!"

"That's what they say." Drew continued to study her. "What's his name?"

Meg studied *him*, uneasiness creeping into her stomach.

"What does it matter?" Clara scowled at the ceiling. "He didn't come."

Meg's eyebrows shot up. "You expected your love interest to come running because you pitched a fit here at the house? How would that work? Unless he was—" She broke off, suddenly aware of a distant whine cutting through the night. Clara sat up like somebody'd pinched her, her face alight with joy.

"Oh my God," Meg said. "You didn't."

"I sure did." She beamed. "And it worked." She bounced off the bed and over to the mirror hanging askew on the wall. She raked her fingers through the sleek curtain of her hair and pinched her already pink cheeks. Her eyes glowed like dark stars and she spun to face Meg. "How do I look?"

"Tragic," Meg said honestly. "Beautiful."

"Awesome." She bounced and hugged her elbows. "I can't believe it worked!"

"What worked?" Drew frowned at her, then shot to his feet. "Oh holy hell, I hear sirens. The cops came after all."

"Exactly," Meg said. She crossed her arms and watched Clara all but dance in place.

"This is a good thing?" Drew asked cautiously.

"No," Meg said.

"Yes," Clara said. "This is a very good thing."

"Do you mind if I ask why? Because I'm going to be honest with you. Every time the cops come to my house, I get arrested."

Meg rolled her eyes at him. "That's the strippers and the scotch talking."

"Yeah, I know." Drew gave a nostalgic sigh. "Man. Those were the days."

"Nobody's getting arrested," Clara told him.

"So why are the cops coming?"

"Because," Meg said. "Apparently Clara's got a crush on a boy in blue, and he's playing hard to get. And if the mountain won't go to Mohammed—"

"—Mohammed will go to the mountain," Clara said smugly.

"Wow," Drew said, his eyes round. "Got to admit it. That's a hell of an encore."

Clara grinned. "Thanks."

Chapter 6

Drew shook his head, half admiring, half astonished. This girl was a piece of work. He wondered if she always had been, or if she'd grown into it.

"Yeah, hell of an encore," Meg said darkly. "So long as you don't mind the part where Mom *gets arrested*."

"Oh, please." Clara waved this away like a stray hair. "*I* wrecked the place. Why on earth would anybody arrest *Mom*?"

"For violating the *restraining order*, Clara." A muscle leapt in Meg's jaw and Drew was suddenly grateful for his brothers. They'd had their differences, sure, but nothing that couldn't be solved with a good punching. Apparently sisters didn't settle things with their fists. Even when they should. Like now.

Meg said, "Mom's not supposed to come within fifty yards of you without Dad's permission, and you know it."

"Um, yeah," Drew said, "about that." He paused delicately and gave Meg the lifted eyebrows.

She said, "Joe doesn't have what you'd call an open mind about Mom's, ah, gifts."

"I see." Drew considered this. "And this didn't come up pre-marriage and kids?"

She shrugged. "Mom was a late bloomer."

Drew would bet good money there was a story behind that terse little sentence but he didn't push. "And when she did eventually bloom?"

"Irreconcilable differences." Meg's smile was blinding. "*The Parent Trap* style."

"Whoa, really?" Drew blinked. "One twin per parent?"

"Co-parenting wasn't really an option. Joe's worldview

30

hinges on Mom being either crazy or a liar—"

"—and the fact that Mom can keep me as level as the drugs screws with his head, hardcore." Clara sighed indulgently. "He doesn't deal well with cognitive dissonance, poor guy. But, Drew, a girl needs her mom. So sometimes I just take a little—" She fluttered graceful fingers. "—medication vacation."

"You go off your drugs?" Drew asked, shocked.

"What else am I supposed to do?" Clara widened her eyes and pressed both hands to her heart. "What kind of father would deny a child in crisis her mother?"

"Our kind." Meg's mouth was hard. "So Clara wrecks her room, Mom comes to smooth her out, and Joe loses his shit. Lather, rinse, repeat. Eventually Dad took out a restraining order." Meg folded her arms and gave her twin a hard look. "Not that Clara cares."

Clara rolled her eyes. "Simmer down there, *pretty Meg*."

Twisting the knife, Drew realized. He just couldn't quite see the actual knife she was twisting. Was she implying that Meg wasn't pretty? Or just not as pretty as Clara was? Either way, it was bullshit. Even if he *could* think when Meg smiled at him—which he usually couldn't—the girl had cameras in her earrings and a bug in her bra, both wirelessly transmitting to her mobile phone. All of which she'd programmed herself. He was getting hot just thinking about it. Throw in the endless legs and he was in serious danger of embarrassing himself.

"Nobody's getting arrested," Clara said airily. "I'll explain everything to the nice officer."

"You will?" Drew glanced around the ruined room. "How?"

"The usual." She gave him the sad, serious eyes he'd first met on the Staircase of Clara. "Bad divorce, over-protective daddy, absent mother—"

"For Christ's sake, Clara," Meg snapped. "There's a *restraining order*."

"—separated from my own *twin*, for goodness' sake." Clara laid the back of one tiny hand to her forehead.

31

"Sometimes it gets to be too much, and I just open the door."

Drew's brows shot up. "The door?"

"Yeah." She pushed splayed fingers through her hair and let it drift back to her shoulders in a silky cloud. "I really do have a mood disorder, you know."

"I never imagined you didn't," Drew told her solemnly. "Tell me about the door."

"When I'm off my meds, it's a little chaotic in my head. Evidently, I have a lot of extra emotion or energy or sensitivity or whatever." She gave a delicate sigh. "More than other people have, or so they tell me."

"Okay." Drew accepted Clara's exceptionalism with an if-you-say-so shrug. "And when you're off your meds, the extra is just, what, all over the place?"

"Right. Messy. Resulting in something very like the floor show I put on here tonight."

"The real deal is scarier, though," Meg put in. "Because she really is unhinged instead of just playing at it."

"But when I'm on my meds," Clara went on, unperturbed by the unsolicited commentary, "all the extra stays behind this door in my head. It's red."

"The extra?"

"The door. Mom gave it to me when I was little."

Drew sneaked a look at Meg. He'd love to know what she believed when it came to her mom. To what her mom could do, or claimed to do. "How do you mean, she gave it to you?"

Clara fell silent. The siren was louder now, closer. It would be ripping into the drive any minute but Clara just looked at him. "Where do you stand on Mom?" she said finally. "On what she can do?"

"I know she fixed my family," Drew said simply. "I don't know how. I just know she did."

"Then you know more than my dad does." Clara's mouth curdled, went briefly hard and ugly. Then it smoothed back to beauty. It was disorienting. "I don't know exactly how it works myself. She just goes quiet and reaches in."

Drew nodded. He'd seen it himself. "And when she's in?"

"It's like cleaning your room," Clara told him. "Suddenly, you can just scoop up all the crap, throw it into the closet and slam the door."

"The red door."

She smiled faintly. "Right. Before she reached in, though, I didn't know how to find the red door. I didn't even know there *was* a red door. She taught me how to find it. How to *make* it, if I couldn't find it." She paused. "It was never locked, though. I could get into it whenever I wanted. Put things in, take things out. I controlled the door, see? Not the other way around. But when I take my meds?" She shook her head. "Locked tight."

Drew said, "But you went through the door just tonight."

"Sure did."

He cocked a brow. "I thought you said you weren't off your meds."

"Oh, well. I'm not." She tossed her hair. "Not completely."

Meg pressed a thumb to the line between her brows. "Clara, my God."

"What? I'm taking them. Just not *all* of them." She shrugged. "I don't mind the door. I just don't like it locked."

"I still don't get why we're here," Meg said. "How does Mom help you entrap a cop?"

"I'm not entrapping him," Clara said loftily. "I'm simply giving him the opportunity to see me in a different light."

Drew blinked at her. "A mentally ill light," he pointed out.

"A fragile light," Clara corrected. "And people who are drawn to police work are saviors. They *love* fragile girls."

"You really want that?" Meg asked, disgusted. "You really want somebody who thinks you're breakable?"

"I want *him*," Clara said, her jaw tight, her eyes hard.

"And what Clara wants," Meg murmured, shaking her head.

Clara only smiled. "Clara gets."

The sirens—now a scream—cut out abruptly. Drew

nudged aside the curtains. "Looks like what Clara wants just pulled into the drive."

"Showtime." Clara gave one last little boogie and skipped out the door. The entire room wilted a bit at her exit, as if somebody had turned the volume down on reality. Or turned it back down to a normal, manageable level. Meg didn't say anything, and Drew found he didn't care for her silence. For the carefully contained quality of it.

"So," he said finally. "I like your family."

"Thank you." She shifted her eyes to him, and they were cool. Still. Remote. Drew didn't care for that, either. "I do, too."

"Do you, pretty Meg?" He couldn't resist throwing the words out there. It wasn't that he wanted to hurt her, but this deliberate distance she'd inserted between them rubbed him the wrong way. Clara was the head case. He was the guy who couldn't stop thinking about the bug in her bra. "Do you really? Because your sister seemed like kind of a nut job."

Meg quirked a brow, perfectly controlled, faintly amused. Unfamiliar temper rose up in Drew, hot and startling. He was getting damn tired of being dismissed by her. "Is that any way to talk about the mentally ill?"

"She's not mentally ill. She's *fragile*." He didn't bother to make the finger quotes; he knew Meg would hear them.

"Fragile." She threw the ceiling a glance so brief that it almost didn't exist. But Drew caught it. He caught it and he knew it for what it was. An eye roll. A blanket condemnation of men, and their panting eagerness to follow the dick wherever it pointed. Even crazy-town. The doorbell pealed and she sighed. "I almost feel sorry for him."

"For who?"

"For Officer Whoever at the door." She shook her head, earrings dancing. "He doesn't stand a chance."

"Wow." Curiosity slid under that lick of temper, pressed it down and pushed it back. He stepped forward to get a better look at her face. To see if that bitter amusement held up to closer inspection. "Are you really that jaded, or do you just not like us?"

She arched a brow. "Not like who?"

34

He tipped his head and frowned at her. Moved closer. "Men," he murmured. He was close enough to touch her now. To smell her.

"Of course I like men." She slanted him a cool smile. "I liked your brother a lot."

"Yeah, you did." He sent her a smile right back, only his was genuine. Because, damn, he liked this girl. He was getting too close, getting in her way. Doing it on purpose, too. But she didn't get whiny about it. She pulled her pins and tossed in the hand grenades. He had to admire that. "Sorry it didn't work out."

"Yeah, well." She gave an airy shrug. "Turns out he likes 'em short and curvy. Not in my wheelhouse, obviously. What can you do?"

Drew had a few ideas. He moved in closer yet. She smelled incredible. Cool and practical and clean on the surface but there was something else underneath. Something hot and complex and just barely there. Something hidden, like that bug in her bra.

And, oh hell, now lust sparkled into the mix. Desire bubbled merrily into the temper and the curiosity. And Drew knew that he was about to do something stupid. Something impulsive. Something really fun and possibly dangerous, not that he'd ever been able to tell the two apart. He opened his mouth with no real idea what might come out.

"It wasn't the short and curvy so much," he heard himself say. "Though Audrey nailed that, no question. No, what laid him out? What finished poor Will right off? It was the straightforward, the fearless and the hot as hell."

"Two out of three," Meg murmured. "I was so close."

"Yeah," Drew said, rolling with it. Enjoying her. "You might've had him if you weren't such a coward."

Her eyes flashed hot and narrow and he thought, *Score*. He'd finally hit her somewhere it hurt. She didn't think she was pretty, but she definitely thought she was brave.

She opened her mouth, a stinging retort surely on her lips, but he jumped in ahead of her. "To be fair, I don't think anybody knew—least of all Will—that that was his holy trinity until Audrey Bing came along. Love's funny like

35

that."

"Love." Now her mouth curdled, proving that she shared more with Clara than just a lightning bolt smile. Drew didn't know how he felt about that. "Love isn't funny."

"Doesn't have to be, no." He took that last step, reached out and snagged her around the waist. Brought her right up into his body, just slid her into place like they were a couple of puzzle pieces. She was long and slim and shocked against him, and everything in his brain fuzzed up and blanked out. *Thank you, Jesus, for tall girls.* "Sometimes it's just fun."

And he kissed her.

Chapter 7

Meg's mind unhinged from her previously scheduled reality and took a bender into I'm-sorry-what-now? territory. She remembered being angry. She remembered being stung. And she remembered opening her mouth to tell Drew exactly where he could stick his self-righteous judgment.

Then suddenly she was in his arms.

He hadn't grabbed her. She'd have remembered that. She'd have responded appropriately to that. She'd have stomped on his foot, put her elbow in his diaphragm, and coolly informed him that *she* was in charge of whom she kissed, and when.

But he hadn't grabbed her. He'd sort of...slid into her. It was those damn hands, she thought vaguely. She'd expected fast and clever. She'd been *prepared* for fast and clever, for paws and tongues. But ruthless, slo-mo inevitability? That had taken her by surprise.

It had been one step closer, then another, then another, talking the whole time, all inane chatter. Distracting, she realized now. He'd been distracting her, showing her something with this hand so she wouldn't wonder what he was doing with the other. And when he'd finally just drawn her right up against his body, right up into the long, taut, shocking heat of him, he'd sparked a minor riot along her nerve endings. Throw that on top of the smoldering fuse of her temper, and the result had been a momentary break in the fabric of reality.

Or that was what she was calling it anyway. Because this couldn't be real. This wild heat streaking down her thighs, the hot press of his mouth on hers, that wide, capable hand cradling her skull, nudging her to just the right angle so he could—

Oh dear God. Drew did *not* kiss like a cocker spaniel. Drew knew what the hell he was doing. He just put her where he wanted her, and *enjoyed* her. Tasted her, learned her, delighted in her. She didn't know if you could smile and kiss at the same time but if it was possible, Drew was doing it.

And she didn't know what to make of that. Didn't know what to make of him. Then he got serious with that arm around her waist and lifted her more fully into him. Into the solid heat and the unapologetic want of him. And rational thought spun away, leaving him. Only him. And Meg dove in.

She slid her fingers into the thick disaster of his hair and it was like living silk in her hands. It wrapped itself around her palms, and she let it tangle her up. She boosted herself onto her toes, met him on his own level and slid right into him. He made a noise, something low and pleased and startled, and she smiled into it. She tasted him, breathed him in, devoured him.

She pushed him back until they hit the wall. Then those big hands were on her hips, snugging her into the thrust and need of him, pulling her into the rhythm of his want. He pressed against her like glory, and the shock waves slid down her legs, pulsed in her stomach. She rolled herself into him, picking up the beat and adding her own. He inched his back down the wall until they were absolutely aligned, want to want. She found herself straddling his thighs, her palms pressed to the wall on either side of his head, their breath tangling together, their mouths clinging and seeking and demanding. His hands slid from her hips to the curve of her bottom, pulling her up, in. Putting her exactly where he wanted her. Where she wanted to be.

But how did he know, she wondered wildly? How did he know *exactly* where she needed him? How did he know how fast, how hard, how eager? How was he *matching* her this way?

It was a stray thought but it had mean little hooks in it. Claws. And they caught. They snatched at the flailing reins of her reason and knotted them together, if tenuously.

Sex wasn't like this. Not any sex Meg had ever had, anyway. This was something new, something different, something dangerous. Nothing you should play with.

She drew back, broke the kiss, dropped her forehead to his shoulder. She didn't have command of her feet just yet, nor was she confident that her knees would hold her up if she managed to step back. It was a start, though. Taking her mouth back. But Drew's hands were still hot on her bottom, and he rolled against her like the tide.

"Oh," she managed. "I—" She broke off, swallowed. "God, Drew, you shouldn't—"

"Sure I should. Why shouldn't I? Why shouldn't *we*?" He moved against her again, slow and hot and hypnotic. Need bloomed low in her stomach, spiraled out, tugging at her knees and fuzzing her resolve. She made a pained noise.

"Christ, Meg, you feel so good." His mouth touched her temple, warm and sweet. He drifted those lips along her cheekbone, dropping tiny kisses all the way to her jaw. She found herself tipping her head to give him room. "So damn good."

But there was a laugh in his voice, a slim thread of amusement under the words. Uncertainty stirred inside her, swirled around with the want and the fear. She drew back to get a better look at that long, angular face. And found him grinning down at her.

He said, "More," and moved in for it.

She drew back. "Yeah, I don't think so."

"Aw. Why not?"

"Because." She scowled up at him. "You're *laughing*."

"Well, yeah." He dropped his head back against the wall and sighed happily. "Because that was *awesome*." He wriggled against her like a puppy, all squirming delight. "Come on, Meg, let's try it again. I want to see if it's as much fun without the element of surprise."

"Fun." She repeated the word mechanically. "You thought that was fun?"

"Didn't you?"

"No." That kiss had been a lot of things. A *lot* of things, most of them hot, slippery and oh-my-Jesus terrifying. But fun? "No, I wouldn't call it that."

"Ah, well." He shrugged cheerfully. "Second time's the charm, right?"

"No, the third time's the charm. The second time is just the second time."

"Looks like we're behind, then. You should definitely kiss me again." He grinned at her, this time slow and hot and dark. "In the name of science."

She considered him. Considered that mouth, those eyes, those slow, shifty hands. "Science, huh?"

"Think of it as the control group." His eyes dropped to her mouth. "Come on, pretty Meg. Kiss me."

Need twisted inside her, tightened and held. "I really wish you'd stop calling me that."

"Stop being so damn pretty, then." Heat licked into his voice, slid under all that amusement like an undertow. "Kiss me again, Meg." The amusement went sly. Knowing. "I dare you."

"You dare me." She snorted. "God, Drew. Really?"

"Really." His hands eased into the small of her back, rested there warmly. Encouragingly. "You're not afraid, are you?"

She was terrified. "Please." She rolled her eyes but leaned forward a scant inch. Two. Right into the hot zone. Jesus, her nerves wanted to sizzle right out of her skin. "But I am going to kiss you again."

"You are?" His brows popped up even as his palms settled more firmly into the dip of her spine. Nudged her closer.

"I am, but not because you dared me."

"No?"

"Of course not." She stopped herself an inch from that mouth, when she could feel his breath on her lips. She pressed her palms to the wall on either side of his shoulders. Reminded herself not to grab him by the hair this time. "This is for science."

And it was. He'd just blown up her entire nervous system, after all. She had to know what part surprise had played in that. Her sanity might depend on it. Her safety certainly did.

"Science." His smile spread. "Okay, sure."

She frowned at him. "Just so you know."

"I do. Just like I know that kissing should involve less talking. And more kissing."

"Right."

Eyes open this time, brain in sharp focus, she took his mouth with hers. And she dared herself to feel it again. Whatever the hell *it* was. Because surely he was right. Surely it had been the surprise that had so completely unglued her like that.

But she was ready for it this time. Ready for him. The second kiss couldn't possibly be as good as the first. It never was.

His mouth softened under hers, warmed. The amusement didn't disappear, only melted into something easy. Inviting. Sweet. Something that rode comfortably alongside the blast of heat and the surge of want that crested inside her the instant her mouth met his. A shock of terror sang through her, and she realized that she'd been wrong. And not only wrong but stupid along with it.

Because the second kiss wasn't as good as the first. It was better. Way better. Exponentially better. Or worse, depending on how you wanted to construct the scale. Because heat she could handle. Lust? Problematic, but okay. Libido was an unpredictable thing and was under no obligation to make sense. But what the *hell* was sweetness doing here, all tangled up inside it? This wasn't fun. This wasn't easy or casual or even just hot. This was serious.

And Meg didn't have a lot of hard-and-fast rules about kissing, but she had one: When and if kissing ever became serious, it should be equally serious for all parties involved. But the man she was kissing, the man who was stirring up all this serious inside her? He was *laughing*. She could hardly breathe for wanting him, but he was still smiling. Oh, not with his mouth or anything. He was kissing her, and with total concentration and a lot of enthusiasm. But she could feel it there, that smile, holding just under the surface, just like always. Drew was hot for her, yes. But not enough to concern him.

And she was all but wrecked.

And that spelled trouble. Serious trouble.

She stepped back. Her knees trembled but held and she folded her arms so she wouldn't reach for him again.

"Aw." Drew sighed, but his eyes danced with that omnipresent amusement. "That's it?"

"Sorry, pal. I'm cutting you off." Her mouth wanted to crumble so she rolled her lips in and bit them. Hard. And ah, Christ, she tasted like Drew. "It's for the best."

"I disagree." He leaned in earnestly, his hair a charming tumble on his brow. "We were on par for *best*, then we hooked it into the rough. You want to walk me through the instant replay?"

She angled him a cool look. "Golf analogies? Really?"

He grinned cheerfully. "You ever play? Lot of common ground between golf and sex."

"And that right there is why we're not having sex." She turned away. "Go make a tee time."

"What are you so afraid of?" he asked softly. "That was some good, clean fun right there, pretty Meg. No need to get all twisted up over it."

And that right there, she thought, was exactly why she *was* all twisted up. Because he was playing games and she was dangerously close to something more.

"Sex isn't a sport," she told him.

"Oh, Meg," he said fondly. "Everything's a sport."

He probably had a point.

"Fine. I don't want to play."

"Really?"

Her brain helpfully replayed a hot and vivid chunk of her recent sensory experience—of his hair wrapped around her palms, of the clinging heat of his mouth, the sweetness of his smile against her lips. Her cheeks went hot—along with other areas of her anatomy best left unmentioned—and she was glad she'd given him her back.

"Okay, fine," he said finally. "You don't want to play. With me, though? Or at all?"

42

"How am I supposed to answer that?" she snapped. "What do you want to hear, Drew?"

"That you've changed your mind," he answered promptly. "That you'd like to take a mulligan. That it's Naked Olympics time and you're going for the gold. An endeavor, by the way, that I would support you in. Fully. Just say the word and I am *there*."

She barked out a laugh. "Well, I guess I asked for that."

"No, *I* asked for that. You said no." He sent her an appealing smile. "I'm just looking for some wiggle room between the n and the o. Because we nailed the qualifying round, Meg. *Nailed* it. Seems like a shame to pull out now."

"That's what she said," Meg murmured before she could help herself.

His smile went brilliant. "Well, that tears it. Now you're going to have to marry me."

She stared at him, momentarily shocked beyond speech. Then she sighed. "The passing urge to bone a girl isn't really grounds for a marriage proposal, Drew."

"The urge is rarely passing, Meg," he said seriously.

She laughed in spite of herself. Trust Drew to be both brutally honest and sort of funny at the same time. She said, "This would be a lot easier if I didn't actually like you."

He cocked his head. "You like me?"

"Go figure." She shrugged. "You're growing on me."

"I like you, too." He paused. "I would also very much like to see you naked. I don't think the two are unrelated."

"I do. You're a guy." She shook her head ruefully. "You want to see everybody naked."

"Well...yes." He considered that. "That's true, I do."

She laughed again, and with near-genuine amusement. "You don't take anything seriously, do you?"

"Not if I can help it."

Again with the truth. God, this guy was dangerous. He simply would not lie to her, no matter how many opportunities she gave him. And she really wanted him to lie to her. It would be so much easier to stick to *no* if he would just start giving her a better reason than fear.

That said, she could work with this.

"Yeah, see, that's the thing," she told him. "I do. I take things very seriously. Including kissing. Naked kissing, especially."

"Ah." He sobered. "You were planning to take me...seriously?"

"No." She shook her head. "I wasn't. I'm not." But she *could*. And if he kissed her like that again, she probably would. Which would be fatally stupid since Drew was patently incapable of returning the favor. "Which is why we're not indulging in any Naked Olympics. Because I take my sporting events seriously."

"Yeah?" He lifted an interested brow. "How seriously?"
She didn't smile. "Very."

He held her gaze for a long, breathless moment. "I could try serious."

Panic sparked inside her, leapt and twirled. "No, you can't." She wrapped her arms around her stomach and turned to face him fully. "You're, what, twenty-one? Twenty-two?"

"Twenty-two."

"There are a lot of women you need to see naked before you get anywhere near serious." He opened his mouth and she lifted a hand. "I'm twenty," she said. "Same goes."

He subsided, mollified if a little sulky about having the sexist argument snatched out from under him. And she liked what sulky did to that mouth of his. She went on before he could launch into his backup wheedle. Before she could get too hung up on his mouth.

"And, yeah, the sex might be awesome. Right up until I punched you for proposing to a pretty stripper or a hot cashier or even to Audrey, if you haven't already. And if I beat Will to the punch, so to speak."

Drew squinted into the distance. "*Have* I proposed to Audrey yet?"

God, he couldn't even remember. "My point," she told him with admirable patience, "is that the sex might be incredible but it wouldn't end well, and that would piss me off. Because I actually like you, Drew."

"You said that."

"Well it keeps surprising me." She lifted a shoulder.

"But my mom communes with spirits, my dad's six-and-a-half feet of scary and my sister's more than a little off her gorgeous rocker. You met them all at their worst and you didn't laugh, faint, or prat-fall into love. Which is why I'm keeping you."

"You are?"

"Yep." She aimed a sharp finger at him. "We're going to be friends."

He stared. "But...Naked Olympics."

"Don't be such a whiner. You can still go for the gold. Just not with me." She waved a vague hand. "Find yourself a flexible little Russian or something."

He folded his arms, dissatisfied. "She won't have a bug in her bra."

"You'll hope not."

A sly smile brushed the dissatisfaction right off that long, interesting face. "Says you."

She shook her head, fought an answering smile. "You're a sick man, Drew."

He eyed her with pity. "How can a girl who kisses like you even say such a thing?"

Heat prickled up her thighs but she only folded her arms. "Forget the kissing. The kissing isn't for us. The kissing was—"

An aberration, she was going to say. A mistake. A figment of your imagination.

Then the shouting started downstairs.

"Oh, hell," she muttered and kissing went clean out of her mind. She bolted for the stairs, Drew right behind her.

Chapter 8

Drew had to give Meg credit. Those legs weren't for show. The girl had speed. He wondered briefly if she'd played basketball or volleyball, then decided she had more of a sprinter's build. Probably track. High school? College? Either way, he was panting by the time he caught up to her on the stairs.

She hit the landing, swung around the newel post, and flew through a sitting room that made Drew think of water colors. She stopped short in the archway on the far wall, likely hoping to get a read on the situation ahead before barging into it. Smart girl. He'd always admired brains. He stopped right behind her, and peered over her shoulder into a kitchen. Lots of honey-toned cabinetry there, and a peninsula counter that divided the room into a cooking space and an eating space. Judging from the track lighting alone, he'd guess that nobody had updated the décor since Hildy used to cook here.

She wasn't cooking now, of course, but Hildy was planted firmly in the business half of the kitchen, triangulated between the stove, the fridge and her weeping daughter. Clara was slumped on her elbows on the peninsula counter, pouring noisy tears onto the Formica. Joe was parked opposite her in a cozily-curtained eating nook, one hip parked on a dining table, fists tight in his elbows while he engaged in a stare-down with the cop in his kitchen.

The responding officer—whom Drew assumed must be Clara's beloved—stood at the apex of the peninsula counter returning the regard with lantern-jawed stoicism. Drew grinned in spite of himself. If they'd called central casting and asked for Aryan Cop #1, this was the guy who'd have turned up. Tall, blond, and pathologically well-pressed, the guy was a dead ringer for Rolfe from *The Sound of Music*. Drew wondered if Clara had been sneaking him into the gazebo out back for song-and-dance numbers after midnight, too. If that's what the kids were calling it these days.

He also wondered if Joe had any idea that his daughter had romantic designs on poor Rolfe. He doubted it, as the guy was still on his feet and at attention, an official-looking document in one hand, a wary eye on Joe.

"Okay," Joe said finally. "All right. Listen, thank you for coming, Officer, but it looks like this has all been a misunderstanding." He pushed off the table and Officer Dreamy's free hand drifted toward the cuffs on his belt. Dreamy was no shorty, but Joe was impressively tall, and his face could cut stone. "It appears that my daughter isn't off her medication, after all. There's no need for you to, ah, execute the, ah—" He nodded significantly toward the paper in the cop's hand.

The cop's jaw went stubborn and Drew was not surprised. Because anybody this well ironed was obviously a rule follower. A T-crosser and an I-dotter. And he was going to see justice served, exactly as spelled out by the paper in his hand.

"I sympathize with your position, sir," Officer Dreamy said with such authority-laden *fuck you* that Drew wanted to punch him on principle. "But as an officer of the law, I'm duty-bound to serve this Temporary Detention Order against one Clara Diana Marshall. You're free to amend your complaint at the hearing."

"Jesus, could you just—" Joe glanced toward his weeping daughter. He stepped toward the officer, his big hands patting the air between them. "—keep your voice down? I'm sure we can work something out—"

"Temporary Detention Order?" Clara's head came up. She turned to the cop, her eyes huge and swimming in confusion. "You're not here about the...noise? I made sort of a scene earlier and I thought maybe the neighbors—"

Officer Dreamy shifted on his shiny cop-shoes, barely met her eyes. "No, ma'am."

47

"Ma'am?" Her voice went high and thready, and fresh tears swam into those eyes. "*Ma'am*? For goodness' sake, Ben. You're allowed to use my name."

Joe said, "He is?" He shifted that iron-hard stare to Officer Dreamy. "You know my daughter, *Ben*?"

"Ms. Marshall and I had a class together at Loudon Community," Ben said to Joe. He didn't even glance at Clara.

"Is that so?" Joe's voice was soft but his mouth was tight.

"We've never met off campus," Ben said quickly. "We only exchanged emails for a team assignment."

"How can you act like it was just an assignment, Ben?" Clara said, her voice a ragged whisper, her eyes awash in betrayal. Drew thought it was a little overdone himself, but he had high standards when it came to theater. He doubted anybody else noticed. "We *revealed* ourselves. We shared our hearts! I told you things I've never told anybody."

"It was a *psychology* assignment." Ben continued to speak straight to Joe. "Which by definition involves discussion of emotions. When I ascertained that your daughter's emotions had become personal rather than academic, I deemed it prudent to cut off contact and did so promptly." His super-hero jaw twitched. "It has no bearing on my ability to discharge my duties as an officer of the law."

"Distancing language." Clara flattened her hands on the counter and gazed sadly at them. "Jargon as a buffer." She shook her head. "Are you really so frightened of me, Ben? Of what we shared?"

Joe's brows came down thunderously. "And what, exactly, did you share?"

"Nothing!" Ben said hastily, "There was no sharing!" He glanced at Clara only briefly before putting his attention back on Joe. "As I stated previously, sir, this is the first time I've seen your daughter outside of class. We've exchanged *emails*, nothing more."

"People fall in love via email all the time." Clara lifted her head to smile softly at him. "All the time, Ben."

"Love?" Officer Ben turned to stare at her, then just hung there, derailed. Drew had to assume he was momentarily stunned by the blunt instrument of her beauty.

"Yes, love." Clara's eyes were Disney-soft on the surface but there was something hard and implacable underneath, and for a moment—a single, weak moment— Drew almost felt sorry for Officer Ben. "Maybe you're too afraid to give voice to what's in your heart, but I'm not. And I've been patient, Ben. So patient. I've given you the time and space to come to grips with your emotions—"

"My—" Ben snapped out of it with a furious gargle. "I *have no emotions* for you, Clara!"

"Aw. Of course you do, sweetheart. It's just a matter of getting in touch with them." Clara smiled serenely. "Which, of course, would be difficult for a personality as dominant and task-oriented as yours. That's why I staged tonight's little intervention. You need to come to grips with your feelings for me, Ben. But how was that going to happen if you wouldn't even talk to me?"

Ben stared, finally beyond words. Drew's little flutter of sympathy grew into an actual pang.

"Wait," Joe said to Clara. "You *staged* this?" His eyes went narrow and he jerked a thumb toward Ben. "For *him*?"

"Of course," Clara said.

"Oh dear," Hildy murmured.

"You *what*?" Ben asked, eyes going sharp and hard.

"She wrecked the house," Joe murmured wonderingly, as if to himself, "so her boyfriend the cop would have to come over."

"I'm not her boyfriend," Ben snapped. "And that's illegal."

"What choice did I have?" Clara spread innocent hands. "You wouldn't take my calls, you were ignoring my emails and texts, you even unfriended me on Facebook." She sighed. "That was childish, Ben. But not unexpected given what we know about the post-adolescent male psyche. You're deeply uncomfortable with powerful emotion." She gave him that silk-over-steel smile that filled even Drew—an innocent bystander—with awe and wonder and a touch of fear. "As are most powerful men. Good cops are always difficult boyfriends." She shrugged. "But when I really thought it through I realized that I could use the cop in you—that thing that was keeping us apart—to bring us together instead." She grinned slyly. "And here you are."

Ben went abruptly dark. His brows came down, his jaw went hard, his lips all but disappeared. Drew thought *uh oh*. Because Ben could take gorgeous women falling willy-nilly into love with him. Ben could handle an on-line stalker. But screwing with his job? Jerking the *badge* around? Ben was clearly having none of that.

"You left me no choice but to organize this meeting," Clara told him in tones of perfect reason. "Because, really, Ben, this degree of denial is unhealthy. It's time to address the elephant in the room."

"I agree," Ben said, and pinned her with blue eyes that contained a whole lot of distance and not much else.

"You do?" Clara clasped her hands to her chest and beamed.

"Absolutely." Ben unclipped the cuffs from his belt and moved toward her. "It's beyond time something was done about it."

"Officer, please," Hildy said, putting out a hand and stepping to Clara's side.

"I'm sorry, ma'am," Ben told her. "But what your daughter's just admitted to is a crime."

Clara's radiant bloom wilted into confusion. "But I only—"

"A crime that I will be reporting to the judge at her hearing." He gave Hildy his profile and turned to Clara. "Clara Diana Marshall," he said, "I will now be taking you into custody and escorting you to the nearest medical facility where you will undergo a three-day mental health evaluation, as requested by your father and so ordered by the magistrate."

There was a moment of explosive silence.

Joe said, "Shit."

Clara said, "As requested by my *father*?"

Hildy said, "Oh dear."

Meg sighed, a barely perceptible up-and-down of her shoulders.

Clara turned on Joe with smoking rage. "*You* requested the TDO on me?"

To Joe's credit, he didn't flinch. "Yes."

Her laugh was sharp with disbelief. "You'd have your own daughter committed?"

"Not committed," Joe said tightly. "Evaluated. A TDO isn't a life sentence, Clara. It's just what it says—a temporary detention order. It's a few days in the hospital to get you back on your meds and leveled out—"

"Except that I'm not *off* my meds!"

"Well, I know that *now*." Joe's mouth was a bitter line. "But yesterday? The day before that? The *month* before that? What was I supposed to think? You were throwing tantrum after tantrum like a goddamn two-year-old who wanted her mommy!"

"I *did* want my mommy!"

"You *needed* your meds!"

"They aren't interchangeable, Dad! The meds can't replace my mother!" Clara threw him a look of burning hatred. "And neither can you."

He drew back like she'd slapped him. For one frozen instant they stared at each other, then Joe lowered his head. Color rushed into his cheeks and the muscles in his forearms rippled like water.

"We discussed this, Clara," he said. "We agreed that if you could be med-compliant for six months, we would revisit the restraining order."

Ben and his cuffs paused. "Restraining order?"

"Daddy dearest took out a restraining order against my own mother," Clara told him. "Nice family dynamics, huh? That's why I'm taking psych classes. What's your excuse?" She didn't wait for an answer, only turned a magnificent glare on her father. "And I *know* what I agreed to. But guess what? I fell in love—"

Ben made a pained noise.

"—and I needed to see my *mom*."

"Why?" Joe folded his arms like a guy who'd much

rather put a fist through the wall instead. He jerked his chin toward Ben. "This guy doesn't want you, Clara. Any idiot can see that. He's here to arrest you." She only glared at him, and Joe glared back. "And guess what? Your mom can't make him love you any more than she can make you well. She's *not magic*, Clara. She's selfish. She gets her jollies out of convincing people—sad, vulnerable, broken people—that she can make them feel better. But she can't. She only makes *herself* feel better, and takes their money to boot."

"Oh, Joe," Hildy said sadly. "Is that really what you think?"

"Goddamn it, Hildy, what am I supposed to think?" Joe's control slipped and he surged forward, slapped both palms down on the counter and leaned in. "Just what the hell am I supposed to think?"

Ben's hand went to his cuffs again. "You're going to want to calm down, sir."

"No, I'm going to say this." Joe stalked around the peninsula to get at Hildy, and Officer Ben practically skipped in his haste to get out of the way. Drew suppressed a snicker. He wondered when ol' Ben would notice that Joe had just owned his ass, and cuff somebody to compensate.

Joe ignored him like the alpha he clearly was. He just kept steaming until he'd put himself right between Clara and Hildy like a shield, as if to protect his child from the poison that was her mother.

He glared down at his ex-wife—he probably had her by a solid foot—and said, "You're the mother of my child, Hildy, and I've tried—God knows I've tried—to keep our differences away from her. But I'm drawing the line right here." His hands were in fists on his hips, and he pushed the words out through his teeth.

"Dad!" Clara latched onto his elbow and tugged. "Dad, stop it! You're being a jerk!"

Joe shook off his daughter as easily as a horse flicking flies. "You're a fraud, Hildy." He threw the words at her like stones, sharp and small. "You're a con artist, and you prey on the vulnerable."

"I help people find peace," Hildy said quietly. "I help

them get their hands around their grief so they can put it away. How is that wrong?"

"It's wrong because you're selling a product that doesn't exist. You're telling them you can do something that you can't. Nobody can. And to take their money on those conditions only compounds the wrong. But to do it to your own child? *Our* child? Our vulnerable and ill child? That makes you a monster, Hildy. A goddamn monster."

Hildy stood as if frozen, simply gazing at her husband—her ex-husband, Drew reminded himself. Because they sure fought like they were still married. She didn't move, didn't flinch, but that trademark air of utter openness? That radical willingness to hear and receive anything a person offered up? It was crushed. Crushed under the weight of Joe's words and the flood of his contempt.

Drew wondered if he could get away with punching Joe *and* the cop. Just on principle. Then Clara beat him to it.

"Shut up!" She threw herself forward, shoved at her father with both hands and all her weight. She couldn't weigh that much, not by Drew's calculations, but surprise evidently counted for a lot. Joe took an awkward step sideways and stared at his daughter, shocked.

Meg lunged forward but Drew caught her elbow. He wasn't about to let her tag into the match now. Drew's education had been unconventional at best but when it came to impending violence, he had a finely calibrated barometer. And Clara had just buried the needle.

Plus this was what he was here for, right? To put himself between the punchers, and hopefully calm the choppy familial waters? Drew didn't take every job that came his way—he took very, very few of them, actually— but the ones he did take? They got done. Every time. This one would, too.

Meg stopped short at his touch and gave him a terse nod. Message received. His relief was intense but short lived because Meg didn't stand down. She just changed direction and glided silently into the now-empty eating nook instead. Where they were perfectly positioned to keep all the players in clear view of Meg's earring-cam.

A bolt of admiration and desire lanced through him at the realization. And suddenly he didn't care what Meg said about friendship and skipping the Naked Olympics. He was going to kiss this girl stupid at the first possible opportunity. After which she would surely slap his face or shred him with that acid-sharp tongue of hers but damn. It would be worth it. Meg's brand of awesome didn't come along every day.

"You shut your mouth!" Clara shrieked again, her rage huge and sudden. It billowed into the room as palpably as smoke, pushed out all the oxygen and shriveled the light. And Drew thought *oh, hell, she opened the red door.* "Stop yelling at my mother!"

She swung at Joe wildly, landed a shot to his shoulder. It did absolutely no damage but she followed it up with a solid shove, quick as a striking snake.

Joe stumbled back and Meg said, "Oh shit."

Drew thought, *Shit, indeed.* He watched it unfold as if in slow motion—Joe's knee going one way, his weight going another, a second awkward step that tangled his foot up with Hildy's...and here came the elbow. He threw it up hard, obviously flailing for balance. Drew could see that. Any idiot could see that. But then that elbow clipped Hildy's chin and she went down like a sack of oatmeal. Wrong place, wrong time, lights out.

Joe, on the other hand, caught his balance just fine and righted himself. And stood there, six-and-a-half feet of stunned disbelief, staring down at the soft lump of his former wife on the kitchen floor.

Clara's scream all but shattered the windows. There were no words, it was just an inarticulate, consuming house fire of rage. She leapt at her father, teeth bared, hands clawed, hissing fury and violence.

Meg said, "*Shit.*"

And leapt into the fray.

Chapter 9

Meg didn't have a plan. She had facts. Three of them, to be precise.

Fact number one: Joe—for all his faults—would never hit a girl. Not on purpose, anyway. Meg had never seen anything like the bleak horror on her father's face when he realized he'd clocked her mom, and he hated Hildy with a burning passion. His love for Clara was the equal and opposite force balancing his mental scales—or so Meg had always assumed—so the chances of his taking Clara down on his own were slim to none.

Fact number two: Clara desperately needed to be taken down. She'd ripped her little red door right off its hinges and was officially lost to reason. Meg had seen this before. They all had. It was like a seizure. She'd rage until she literally exhausted herself and had to sleep the clock around. Until that happened, she was dangerous as hell.

Which led Meg inescapably to fact number three: With Joe incapable and Hildy unconscious, the dirty work was up to Meg. Unless the cop beat her to it. She suspected *he'd* cold-cock Clara, and happily—could anybody really blame him?—but Meg preferred to keep the punching in-house. What was family for, after all? If the situation were reversed, Clara would do it for her, no question.

So Meg launched herself into the elbows and fists, into the snarling and the sweating. Clara windmilled both arms, a little machine of hurt aimed at Joe. She was hardly being scientific about it but when it came to fisticuffs, quantity often counted for more than quality. Which Meg learned the hard way when Clara missed Joe entirely but landed a good one right on Meg's ear. For a brief moment, she saw stars and heard bells.

"Damn it, Clara," she said and wedged a shoulder between her sister and her father. She wound up sandwiched between them, attempting to straight-arm Joe to a safe distance while Clara lunged against her back, screaming like a harpy over her shoulder. Lucky for Meg, her sister was screaming into the ear she'd just clocked so Meg could barely hear it. "Knock it off!"

Then Joe's arms came around them both in a strangling bear hug, like a weary boxer leaning into the clinch. Meg's arms collapsed, trapped uselessly against her chest. Clara— clearly not into being restrained by the object of her fury— only screamed louder. As an added bonus, Meg's lungs felt like they'd just been compressed by half.

"Gah," she wheezed. "Dad. I've got this. Let go!"

Clara continued to writhe and flail, attempting to climb Meg like a tree, and with remarkable success, too, given Joe's bear hug. Meg had to concede that her sister's manicure was both pretty and a deadly fucking weapon. They swayed there, the three of them, locked in battle for an endless and indeterminate amount of time. Meg squirmed desperately for air and position for what might've been seconds, minutes or decades. At the end of it, however, she had succeeded in reversing herself, so she was facing her howling twin instead of her stoic father.

She let Clara scream (into what would've been cleavage on a normally endowed woman but was actually Meg's bony sternum) while she drove an elbow backward into her father's gut. His breath whooshed out with a hard huff. She took advantage of his surprise to bring her arms together and shoot them over her head. She brought her elbows down sharply on Joe's forearms, and broke his grip.

Meg gave Clara a mighty shove and her twin sprawled back into the counter, panting like something wild and trapped. Meg whirled to do the same to Joe, only to find him struggling to dislodge Drew, who'd apparently leapt onto her father's back and was now clinging like a demented monkey.

Not a bad move, she thought reluctantly. Joe and Drew were of a height, but Drew hadn't yet acquired the forty-ish pounds of muscle that Joe had spent the last couple decades earning. Meg doubted Drew was on track to catch up, either, not with that *subtle* build of his. And since overpowering Joe wasn't a reasonable possibility, Drew had evidently decided to just ride him like a bronco until he calmed down. Drew grinned at her over Joe's shoulder, and she realized he was having the time of his life.

"Still got my moves," he panted. "Miss the strippers and the scotch, though."

The remark must've been just random enough to cut through the last of Joe's adrenaline. He stilled and said, "What?"

Meg gave a short laugh. "If we're not in custody by dawn, I'll buy you a lap dance and a shot down at Maxwell's, how's that?"

"Sounds like a date to me, pretty Meg."

Drew cocked his head, considered the lack of fight on Joe's part, then hopped down. He gave Joe an apologetic pat on the back and took a prudent—large—step back. "Sorry, Mr. Marshall. Meg looked like she was getting hammered in there. So I deployed a non-violent intervention tactic on her behalf."

"Yeah, I got that." Joe rolled a shoulder and eyed him with disgust. "You fight like a girl."

"No, I'm pretty sure your girls could kick my ass." He grinned without a trace of shame. "Individually or as a team."

Joe threw an assessing look Meg's way. "You're probably right."

"I so often am." Drew circled around to stand next to Meg, giving Joe a nice, wide berth.

On the floor Hildy stirred. Joe dropped to his knees like he'd been shot, but his hands were fast and gentle. They slipped under Hildy's head as she moved to sit up, eased her upright, then danced over her hair and under her jaw. "My God, Hildy," he said "I'm so sorry. I didn't mean...it was an accident...Oh hell, are you hurt?"

He sounded near tears. Meg had to look away. She turned her back on her parents, only to find Clara face-down on the counter, her wrists jacked up practically to her shoulder blades while the cop fumbled for those cuffs he'd been fingering all night. She wasn't fighting him, wasn't even crying. She was just lying across the counter like a rag doll, exhausted and spent, her hands limp in the cruel bracket of Ben's fist.

Drew said, "Easy there, crime fighter." He ambled forward but wisely didn't lay a finger on the cop. Evidently, he *did* have his moves still. Meg hadn't done any time in a bar brawl herself but she'd watched her share of cop shows. You never so much as pointed at a cop without risking the dreaded *assaulting an officer* arrest. He went for Clara instead.

"Stand back," Ben snapped.

"Come on, dude," Drew said mildly. He stroked a long swish of black hair away from Clara's damp cheek and cupped a sympathetic palm around the curve of her skull. She snuffled pathetically into the counter. "She's down for the count. Give the cuffs a rest, huh?"

Ben ripped the cuffs free from his belt finally and flipped one open. "Sir, I need you to step away from the sus—"

"Suspect?" Drew finished for him. He met the guy's eye directly. "This isn't a suspect. This is a girl who liked you too much and had a hard time taking no for an answer. Cut her some slack, huh, Ben?"

"*Officer*." Ben's jaw ticked. "And she deliberately created a disturbance and called it in, which makes her—"

"Troubled," Drew said easily. "Mentally ill. Which is why you're actually here, if I'm not mistaken. You didn't even know about the noise report until she told you about it. *Herself.* You were dispatched to help a sick girl get the care she needs." He dropped his eyes deliberately to Clara, whimpering on the counter. "And you're jacking the shit out of her shoulders, so ease up, Officer—" He glanced at the name badge on Ben's chest and barked out a startled laugh. "—Skrewd?" His eyes went bright. "Your name is *Ben Skrewd?*" He laughed as only Drew could, completely delighted with the world and everybody in it. He threw a

58

dancing look Meg's way. "Your sister's *been screwed* by Officer Ben Skrewd! Oh my God. What were the chances of that?"

Ben's jaw went stony and he released Clara's wrists. She didn't even open her eyes, only let out a sigh of relief and curled her arms under her body like broken wings. He stepped right into Drew's face, practically chest-bumped him, and snarled, "Watch it, son, or you might find yourself on the counter next."

Drew's grin only grew. "Wow, that's a generous offer, Officer Skrewd, but when it comes to getting screwed, I generally prefer girls." The grin didn't dim a single watt, but it went hard, fierce. "And I prefer them willing. The crying and cuffing just doesn't do it for me." He didn't so much as glance at Clara on the counter. "Be nice if you could say the same, wouldn't it, *Officer*?"

"Drew, don't," Meg said. "You're baiting him."

"Baiting him? Nah." Drew didn't glance at her, either, just kept that hard, ugly smile pinned on Officer Skrewd. "We're just talking. Isn't that right, Ben?"

"We're done talking," Ben said, his cheeks flushed, his eyes cold. He turned back to Clara, and Meg jumped to the side to keep all three of them in range of her earring cameras.

And was instantly glad she did, because Ben seized Clara by the elbow hard enough to jerk her off the counter. She fell to her knees on the tile with a startled cry but Ben yanked her up, flipping open his cuffs with a move Meg would bet good money he'd practiced in the mirror a time or two (hundred). He snapped one circlet onto her wrist and spun her toward the counter to fasten the other.

Clara let him spin her, hard. She lifted her elbow and followed through equally hard. And Meg watched with pride as her sister caught Officer Ben square in the eye socket with her sharp little elbow.

Drew laughed, purely delighted.

"*Fuck!*" Ben slapped a hand to his eye and glared at Clara with an icy rage. His free hand twitched into a quick fist, like he was thinking about taking a swing of his own.

Drew stopped laughing.

He moved like water, like rain, so easily and so smoothly that Meg gaped. Drew wasn't lazy, exactly, but he wasn't what you'd call quick on the trigger, either. And yet before Ben's fist was even fully formed, Drew was in front of Clara, pressing her into the counter with his back. He stood there between Ben and Clara, arms folded, chin lowered, his face full of grave disapproval.

"You weren't about to hit a girl, now, were you, Officer?"

Ben stared at him in hot silence for a full five-count before he mastered his rage. His hand opened and he said, "Step aside, sir."

Drew considered him for a long beat, then slowly shook his head. "I don't believe I will."

"Step aside," Ben barked, his watering eye already swelling, "or you'll be the one in cuffs."

Drew considered that, too. Then he shot both hands forward. Officer Ben leapt backward, one palm out, one hand going to his belt. For what, though? Cuffs? They were still dangling off Clara's wrist. Gun? Pray God no. But Drew only smiled and kept his arms out. "Okay. Cuff me." He arched a brow, taking in Ben's fight-or-flight stance. "Little jumpy, aren't you?"

"Fuck you," Ben muttered, and dug into a pouch on his belt for the cuff keys. He glared around Drew at Clara. "Wrist," he said. She held it out from behind Drew's back.

"Are you okay, honey?" Drew asked over his shoulder. "Your arm? Your knees?"

"Fine," Clara said softly. "My elbow hurts a little."

Meg couldn't help it. She laughed. "Good for you, kiddo."

Ben shot her a poisonous look. "You want to share a pair of cuffs with your boyfriend?"

Drew aimed a look of melting encouragement at her. "Please say yes."

She laughed again—completely involuntarily—and Ben said, "Fine. Have it your way." He freed Clara with an ungentle jerk and snapped the link over Drew's waiting wrist. He dragged Drew over to Meg.

She said, "Wait, what the—"

Then he had the second circlet snapped over her own wrist. He shoved them both toward the door.

"You have the right to remain silent," Ben began and Meg said, "The hell I will!" But Drew nudged her with an elbow and shook his head. He nodded toward the kitchen behind them, and Meg turned. Over her shoulder she could just see Clara kneeling on the floor, an arm across Joe's shoulders, her head snuggled up beside Hildy's. And Meg understood. This was what she'd bought with her arrest. The time and space for her broken family to close the circle, if only for a moment.

As usual, she wasn't in it.

She shut up and let Ben manhandle her into the backseat of his cop car, handcuffed to Drew Blake.

Chapter 10

"And that brings us up to about...now," Drew said to Chief Wharton in that cramped pee-and-coffee smelling police station he knew so well.

The Chief eyed Meg's earrings. "You say you got all this on tape?"

Meg nodded dully. "You can access the playback on my iPhone. It's still in Drew's truck, in a black backpack."

"It's on the newel post in your dad's foyer, actually," Drew said. "I brought it in." Meg blinked at him and he shrugged. "I didn't know if you'd need it."

"That was right gentlemanly of you, Drew," Wharton said with mild surprise.

"I told you. We're reformed." He glanced at the booking desk, where Ben was still pushing that damn pencil. "I do wonder if Officer Skrewd's paperwork will run true to the playback, though."

"Yeah." Wharton said thoughtfully. "Me, too." He leaned back in his chair until it complained pitifully. "Hey, Ben," he called. "Did you know that this little lady here is wearing cameras in her earrings?"

Ben's pencil went still. "No, Chief." He sent them a carefully blank look. Drew returned it in kind. Meg didn't even turn her head. "No, I did not."

"She's a surveillance expert."

"You don't say."

"I do." The chief paused. "People surprise you in this job. Every dang day."

"Yes." Ben eyed them bitterly. "Yes, they do."

Chief Wharton dropped them off in Joe and Clara's driveway half an hour later, all charges magically dropped.

Wharton buzzed his window down and leaned out. "You two steer clear of trouble now, you hear?"

"Yes, sir," Meg said.

"Do my best," Drew added.

Wharton held eye contact for a beat longer than was comfortable. "You might want to aim a little higher, son."

"Right." Drew nodded quickly. "Will do."

"That's what I wanted to hear." Wharton began to buzz up his window. "Y'all get inside now. It's colder than a well digger's ass out here."

"Thank you, sir," Meg said, waving. "We will."

But she didn't move. She stood there in the frigid air, squinting at the faint graying of the eastern sky. Drew was gripped with the powerful urge to lay an arm around those stiff, brave shoulders, to draw her up against his chest and settle the sleek bump of her ponytail under his chin. He wanted to tip up that tough, stubborn jaw and put his mouth on hers, kiss her until she laughed again. He wanted a lot of things, but watching the cold January dawn spread over Meg's face, he knew he wasn't going to get any of them.

"So," he said. "I'm holding you to what you said earlier."

Her eyes snapped to his and she frowned, wary. Damn, he liked this girl. "What did I say earlier?"

"About keeping me. About us being friends." He held her gaze, didn't smile. "If you're denying me the Naked Olympics, you damn well better come through on the friends thing, or I'm going to be pissed." He dipped his chin and gave her some good, solid eye contact. "I still have my moves, you know."

She studied him for a long moment, during which Drew's heart beat harder and more uncertainly than it should have. Finally she said, "I'm not buying you that lapdance."

"Fair enough," Drew said, relief a weird rush that filled his chest. That filled *him*. "It was contingent upon us not being taken into custody, and we were, so I won't hold you to it." He smiled. "But we weren't actually charged with anything, so you should probably at least buy me that drink."

She huffed out a reluctant laugh. "Deal."

He held out a hand and she eyed it warily. "If you try to hug me, I'm going to hit you."

"Like I would even try."

"Don't lie, Drew. You're a hugger."

He grinned easily. "Busted."

"Don't."

"I won't."

She slipped her hand into his and goosebumps broke out over Drew's back. She gave it a brisk shake and let him go. Fast. Drew filed that away for future consideration. A friend who gave him goosebumps.

He could probably deal with that.

For starters.

***

Stay tuned for Meg and Drew's happy ending in TIME FOR TROUBLE, coming January 2015!

The Red Door Reads 'Who's Ben Skrewd?' Novellas

What do you call eleven books covering the gamut of the romance genre—from regency historical to contemporary, to paranormal, urban fantasy and beyond—all releasing on April 15, 2014 (tax day!) and each featuring a Red Door and a mysterious figure named Ben Skrewd? You call it a novella series like none other, all from the fabulous writers at Red Door Reads!

Liberty and the Pursuit of Happiness
by Deb Marlowe
A Half Moon House Series Novella

Hexed by Andris Bear
A Deadly Sins Novella

Dances with Demons by Lori Handeland
A Phoenix Chronicles Novella

Firebird by Linda Winstead Jones
A Columbyana Novella

In the Stars by Ava Stone
A Regency Encounter Novella

Her Muse, Lord Patrick by Jane Charles
A Muses Novella

Cross Springs In Bloom by Caren Crane
A Cross Springs Novella

The Earl's Passionate Plot by Susan Gee Heino

Touch of Trouble by Susan Sey
A Blake Brothers Novella

Reagan's Revenge by Tammy Falkner
A Reed Brothers Novella

Accidentally in Love by Claudia Dain
A More Courtesan Chronicles Novella

You can find out more at the Red Door Reads
website (www.reddoorreads.com) or visit them on
Facebook! (www.facebook.com/reddoorreads)

About the Author

Susan Sey lives and writes in St. Paul, Minnesota, with her wonderful husband, their two charming children and a whole lot of snow. In addition to producing smart, sexy contemporary romances on an annual basis, Susan is also the proud owner of a filthy house, a broken oven and a cranky van whose off-and-on relationship with the check engine light is driving her crackers.

She loves ice cream, her family and happy endings, though not necessarily in that order. She does not enjoy laundry, failure or mowing the lawn, but rises to the occasion as necessary.

Want to connect with Susan? You can find her at www.susansey.com, where it's just a hop, skip and a click to finding her on Facebook, Twitter, the Romance Bandits, Red Door Reads, and signing up for her newsletter.

Or you can just shoot her an email at susan@susansey.com. She loves a good letter.